מסורה

ArtScroll Youth Series®

THANK YOU HASHEM

By Yaffa Rosenthal

Illustrated by
Rabbi Shmuel Kunda

Published by
Mesorah Publications, ltd

אבגדהוזחטיכלמנסעפצקרשת

אספרה שמך לאחי בתוך קהל אהללך, *I will proclaim Your Name to my brethren, in the midst of the congregation will I praise You (Psalms 22:23).*

Thank You, HASHEM, for giving me this precious opportunity to praise and to thank You. שכן חובת כל היצורים לפניך ה' אלקינו ואלקי אבותינו להודות להלל לשבח לפאר ..., *For such is the duty of all creatures before You, HASHEM, our G-d, G-d of our fathers, to thank, praise, laud, extol ... (Sabbath Morning Prayers).*

❁ ❁ ❁

This book was written for my children — Yisrael Meir, Hadassah, Esther Leeba, Avrahom Shalom — and is dedicated in honor of my father and mother — Leon and Rachel Faigenbam לאורך ימים טובים — in everlasting love and appreciation for their love, gentle understanding, and true devotion.

Heartfelt gratitude to my wonderful parents-in-law — Samuel and Miriam Rosenthal, לאורך ימים טובים — for their exceptional dedication and continuous kindnesses.

Sincere appreciation to all who taught me Torah and *Yiras Shomayim*, but my deepest gratitude goes to Rabbi Yosef Fabian, שליט"א, and Rabbi and Mrs. Chaim Tzvi Katz, שליט"א, of Cleveland, Ohio, and to Rabbi Avigdor Miller, שליט"א, who, through their remarkable dedication and enthusiasm, have brought me to a greater realization of the goodness of the Creator.

It is hoped that this little book will bring young minds to an awareness that everything we are and everything we have, are gifts from HASHEM. May this understanding bring our children to begin to observe and discover the constant benevolence of HASHEM, and hopefully feel and even vocalize an appreciation for these endless gifts. דור לדור ישבח מעשיך וגבורותיך יגידו, *Each generation will laud Your deeds to the next, tell of Your mighty acts (Psalms 145:4).*

Chaya Yaffa Rosenthal

FIRST EDITION
First Impression ... September, 1983

Published and Distributed by
MESORAH PUBLICATIONS, Ltd.
Brooklyn, New York 11223

Distributed in Israel by
MESORAH MAFITZIM / J. GROSSMAN
Rechov Bayit Vegan 90/5
Jerusalem, Israel

Distributed in Europe by
J. LEHMANN HEBREW BOOKSELLERS
20 Cambridge Terrace
Gateshead, Tyne and Wear   England NE8 1RP

ARTSCROLL YOUTH SERIES®
THANK YOU HASHEM
© Copyright 1983 by Yaffa Rosenthal, 1424 Avenue R, Brooklyn, NY 11229

Typography by CompuScribe at ArtScroll Studios, Ltd.
1969 Coney Island Avenue / Brooklyn, N.Y. 11223 / (212) 339-1700

Did you ever look up at the beautiful sky?
It is a gift whenever you want it. Do you know why?
Did you ever take a breath of clean, fresh air?
Aaah … It is a gift that is always there.

Did you ever feel the warmth of the strong sun shining?
Did you ever stop to look at the orange sun setting?
These gifts are always there for your pleasure,
and there are many more for you to treasure.

Who gives you these gifts, all these things that you see?
HASHEM made it all. He was, He is, and He always will be.
There is much, much more for you — just look and see.
HASHEM is everywhere, always. So let's all thank Him happily.

ד	ה	ו
י	כ	ל
ס	ע	פ
ר	שׁ	ת

א	ב	ג
ח	ח	ט
מ	נ	
צ	ק	

אוֹר

Light

Thank You HASHEM for bringing me light
so I can see everything just right.

א בגדהוזחטיכלמנסעפצקרשת

בַּיִת
Home

ב

Thank You HASHEM for a wonderful warm home,
where I'm always loved and never feel alone.

גֶּשֶׁם
Rain

ג

Thank You HASHEM for the rain You shower.
It makes the fruits and vegetables flower.

אבגדהוזחטיכלמנסעפצקרשת

דִּבּוּר
Speech

ד

Thank You HASHEM for the words you let me say.
So I can talk when I daven, when I learn, and when I play.

אבג**ד**הוזחטיכלמנסעפצקרשת

הוֹרִים

Parents

Thank You HASHEM for my Mom and Dad,
who teach me the difference between good and bad.

אבגדהוזחטיכלמנסעפצקרשת

וָלָד
Baby

Thank You HASHEM for a baby so cute and small.
Let's watch HASHEM make the baby grow tall.

אבגדהוזחטיכלמנסעפצקרשת

זֶמֶר

Song

Thank You HASHEM for the joy You bring
through the beautiful songs You let me sing.

אבגדהוזחטיכלמנסעפצקרשת

חָבֵר

Friend

Thank You HASHEM for the friend I like.
I share things with him … even my bike!

אבגדהוזחטיכלמנסעפצקרשת

טַעַם

Taste

ט

Thank You HASHEM for making food so delicious,
from ripe fruit to Mommy's favorite dishes.

אבגדהוזחטיכלמנסעפצקרשת

יוֹם טוֹב

Jewish Holidays

ל

Thank You HASHEM for Yom Tov days
that make us so happy in hundreds of ways.

אבגדהוזחטיכלמנסעפצקרשת

כּוֹכָבִים

Stars

כ

Thank You HASHEM for stars, so far away and bright.
They bring excitement and sparkle to the dark night.

אבגדהוזחטיכלמנסעפצקרשת

לֶחֶם
Bread

Thank You HASHEM for bread to make us strong.
We can eat delicious sandwiches all day long.

אבגדהוזחטיכלמנסעפצקרשת

מַיִם

Water

מ

Thank You HASHEM for the water we use in so many ways.
It feels cool and delicious on hot summer days.

א ב ג ד ה ו ז ח ט י כ ל מ נ ס ע פ צ ק ר ש ת

נְיָר

Paper

Thank You HASHEM for paper. With crayons, scissors, or ink,
we can do so much with paper — just think!

אבגדהוזחטיכלמנסעפצקרשת

סְפָרִים
Books

ס

Thank You HASHEM for books from which we learn and discover,
and read and enjoy from cover to cover.

אבגדהוזחטיכלמנ**ס**עפצקרשת

עֵשֶׂב

Grass

Thank You HASHEM for grass — wherever you go there is more.
Run across an open field! You can't buy that in the store.

אבגדהוזחטיכלמנסעפצקרשת

פַּטִּישׁ

Hammer

Thank You HASHEM for the tools You taught us to make,
so we can build new things and fix the ones that break.

אבגדהוזחטיכלמנסעפצקרשת

צַדִּיקִים
Righteous People

Thank You HASHEM for tzaddikim who teach us Torah and lots more.
I try to be like them even though I am only four.

אבגדהוזחטיכלמנסעפ**צ**קרשת

קַיִץ

Summer

ק

Thank You HASHEM for a season in the sun,
when we can learn and play and have such fun.

אבגדהוזחטיכלמנסעפצקרשת

רוּחַ

ר

Wind

Thank You HASHEM for the wind that blows every place.
It feels so fresh and cool on my face.

אבגדהוזחטיכלמנסעפצקרשת

שַׁבָּת

The Sabbath

Thank You HASHEM for Shabbos, the day of holiness and rest.
All Shabbos things are so special; I love it the best.

אבגדהוזחטיכלמנסעפצקרשת

תּוֹרָה
Torah

Thank You HASHEM for the Torah You give
to the Jewish people to show us how to live.

אבגדהוזחטיכלמנסעפצקרשת

Thank You HASHEM for all these beautiful things,
and for all the goodness each new day brings.
Thank You HASHEM for my life, my family, and my health,
and the Torah and mitzvos, my greatest wealth.